THE SUBSTITUTES

by Kathryn Lay
illustrated by Marcos Calo

Calico

An Imprint of Magic Wagon
www.abdopublishing.com

www.abdopublishing.com

Published by Magic Wagon, a division of ABDO, PO Box 398166, Minneapolis, Minnesota 55439. Copyright © 2015 by Abdo Consulting Group, Inc. International copyrights reserved in all countries. No part of this book may be reproduced in any form without written permission from the publisher. Calico™ is a trademark and logo of Magic Wagon.

Printed in the United States of America, North Mankato, Minnesota.
102014
012015

Written by Kathryn Lay
Illustrations by Marcos Calo
Edited by Rochelle Baltzer, Heidi M. D. Elston, Bridget O'Brien
Cover and interior design by Laura Rask

Library of Congress Cataloging-in-Publication Data

Lay, Kathryn, author.
 The substitutes : an Up2U action adventure / by Kathryn Lay ; illustrated by Marcos Calo.
     pages cm. -- (Up2U adventures)
 Summary: Josh and Jenny are disturbed that their school is suddenly overrun with nearly identical substitute teachers who ask strange questions and record everything that the students say--but when their own teacher disappears the twins set out to find out what is going on, and who is responsible, and the reader must choose the solution.
 ISBN 978-1-62402-095-7
1. Plot-your-own stories. 2. Substitute teachers--Juvenile fiction. 3. Schools--Juvenile fiction. 4. Twins--Juvenile fiction. 5. Brothers and sisters--Juvenile fiction. 6. Conspiracies--Juvenile fiction. [1. Substitute teachers--Fiction. 2. Teachers--Fiction. 3. Schools--Fiction. 4. Twins--Fiction. 5. Brothers and sisters--Fiction. 6. Conspiracies--Fiction. 7. Plot-your-own stories.] I. Calo, Marcos, illustrator. II. Title.
 PZ7.L445Su 2015
 813.6--dc23
                                        2014034276

TABLE OF CONTENTS

CHAPTER

→ 1 ←

Questions

Josh reached down to pick up his twin sister's math book. When he straightened, he was staring into the face of another new substitute.

"Uh, sorry Jenny dropped her book on your foot," Josh said.

The substitute stared at him with her bright green eyes. She gave him a smile that sent a chill down his spine. When she smiled, the lobster tattoo on her cheek wrinkled.

"Why did your sister drop her book?" the red-haired woman asked.

Josh backed away. "It was an accident."

"Accident?" the substitute asked.

Josh stared at her. She acted as if the word were new. Suddenly, he was yanked backward by his shirt.

"Let's get to class," his sister whispered.

They walked around the substitute. When Josh looked back, she was still standing in the same spot, talking into a cell phone on her wrist.

"What is going on with these new substitutes?" Josh asked. "There are new ones every day."

Josh and Jenny raced down the quiet halls, past rows of lockers. It was only the second week of fifth grade, and they had already been late three times.

Jenny looked back at him. "They're just spooky. And weird."

Three classroom doors opened at the same time. Three substitutes walked out and stared at Josh and Jenny. Each had red hair and bright green eyes. And each wore gray pants with a blue shirt.

One substitute had a star tattoo, one had a bird, and the other had a frog. Just like all the new substitutes, they each had a long thin cell phone attached to a wristband.

As Josh walked past them, one pointed at him. When she spoke, the bird tattoo on her cheek seemed to move. "Student, please explain how the president is chosen."

Josh cleared his throat. "Um, by election?"

"What is 'by election'?" another sub asked.

"We're late to class," Jenny said.

Josh walked quickly past them. When they reached their classroom, Josh flung open the door.

"Late again, Mr. and Miss Stuard," their teacher said.

"Sorry, Mr. Ott," Josh said, hurrying to his seat. Jenny slid into hers.

Josh was glad to see Mr. Ott standing beside his desk. He was new this year, but everybody liked him.

"Now, before I give you your vocabulary test, I have exciting news," Mr. Ott said.

Josh leaned forward in his seat. Mr. Ott had been hinting they were going to do a special project the first semester. The year before, a teacher had someone bring in animals from the zoo every Friday, and the class got to learn about them. Another teacher turned the classroom into a kingdom, with castle walls, a king and queen, and even a dungeon.

What could Mr. Ott be planning?

"First thing after lunch, we will talk about our new project for the semester."

Josh glanced at Jenny. She frowned. They both hated waiting for things.

After the vocabulary test, Mr. Ott showed a movie about Egypt.

"Hey Josh," a voice whispered in the dark.

"What?" Josh asked. He knew it was Curtis Beamer. Curtis always talked during movies.

"I bet we have more substitutes than regular teachers now," Curtis said.

Josh leaned toward his friend. "Yeah. And what's with all those questions they ask?"

"I know," Curtis said. "It's like we're on a game show."

"Quiet, boys," Mr. Ott said.

Josh leaned back. He watched the clock instead of the movie. Finally the bell rang for lunch. He poked his sister's arm as they hurried out the door.

"What do you think the special project will be?" he asked.

Jenny grinned. "I don't know, but I bet it'll be the best one yet."

After getting their food, Josh and Jenny grabbed their favorite table.

Josh looked around the cafeteria. The new substitutes were everywhere. The regular teachers on lunch duty stood together talking. But the substitutes walked down the rows of tables, stopping every few minutes to lean forward, ask a kid a question, speak into their phone, and walk on to another kid.

Jenny chewed her food and mumbled, "Why won't they leave us alone?"

"Hey, stop spraying your food," said Josh. "I'm going to smell like tuna all day."

Charlie Weatherby leaned across the table. "A substitute actually asked me questions through the bathroom door yesterday."

"Eeew," Jenny said. "Did you answer?"

Charlie shrugged. "I didn't even know the answer to tell him. He asked when the first ship from Earth went into space."

Josh nodded. These substitutes had lots of questions. His cousin said they were the same at his school. They didn't really teach, just asked questions.

Jenny finished her milk and said, "There is something scary and mysterious about them."

Josh and Charlie agreed.

When lunch was over, Josh hurried down the halls back to class. What was Mr. Ott's big announcement? Maybe it would be about building airplanes. No, that would be hard to do in school. Or maybe they would invent a new cookie. He licked his lips as he followed Jenny into the classroom.

Jenny stopped suddenly. Josh ran into her.

"Hey, what's the big idea? Don't hit the brakes without a warn . . ." He looked to where Jenny was pointing.

Standing beside Mr. Ott's desk was a woman. A woman in gray pants and a blue shirt. A woman with red hair. A woman who looked at them with green eyes and had a ladybug tattoo on her cheek.

A substitute.

CHAPTER
→ 2 ←

Kidnapped

Josh stared at the substitute. She stared back.

"Children must return to their seats on time," she said.

Josh slipped into his seat.

"I am your substitute. Your teacher had to . . . go away. I will be your teacher until he returns." She smiled and everyone seemed to gasp at once. "I will need you to tell me what you have been taught."

Josh jumped up. "Where is Mr. Ott? He was here before lunch. He promised he had a surprise to tell us. He wouldn't leave without keeping his promise."

The substitute turned away from Josh as if he hadn't spoken. "Today, you will tell me what you have learned about your history. Who can tell me how this country was discovered?"

Josh fell back into his seat. He looked at Jenny. He touched his nose and winked. She nodded. She knew what to do.

Josh started coughing. But the substitute did not look away from Kaylie Jones, who was talking about Columbus. Ladybug-Sub held her wrist phone closer to her mouth and talked quickly.

Josh coughed louder. He coughed harder.

Jenny waved her arm. "Miss Substitute? My brother is sick."

The substitute stopped talking and turned toward Jenny. "What is wrong with him?"

Josh coughed more.

"It's his allergies. He must have eaten something at lunch that made him sick. I always take him to the nurse when it happens."

The substitute stared at Josh. Her green eyes seemed to get bigger. Then, she smiled her strange smile.

"If the student is sick, the student must see the school nurse."

"Thanks," Josh said. He grabbed Jenny's arm, and they ran out of the room.

"Great job," he told Jenny.

"I was afraid she'd say no or ask about the history of coughing and allergies," Jenny said.

They stood in the hall. There were no substitutes or teachers around.

"I wonder if there are any teachers left in school," Jenny said. "What are we going to do?"

Josh folded his arms. "We're going to look for Mr. Ott. He has to help us find out what's happening."

Jenny followed him down the hall toward the office. "Think about it, Josh. Where is the best place to find a missing teacher?"

Josh turned. "Where?"

"Where else," Jenny said. "The teacher's lounge."

Josh grinned. "Lead on."

They had to walk down three halls and upstairs to get to the teacher's lounge. No kid ever went inside, but everyone knew where it was. Kids liked to talk about the teachers sitting around drinking sodas, eating pizza, and talking about their students.

Josh slid against the wall and peeked around the corner. He looked across the hall past the library toward the stairs.

"Oh great," he said.

"What's wrong?" Jenny asked.

"There's a substitute near the stairs," Josh said. "We have to wait."

Jenny leaned past him to look around the corner. "Hey, what's she doing?"

Josh looked where she was pointing. Miss Fable, the librarian, stood by the library door.

Miss Fable looked both ways down the hall, then motioned toward the substitute.

The red-haired woman walked to the librarian and saluted her. Then she stood very still as Miss Fable spoke quietly.

Josh's mom said he could hear a fly tiptoeing across grass. He leaned over a little and held his breath.

"We must move quickly. People are beginning to get curious," Miss Fable said.

The substitute nodded.

"Take this one to the lounge and into the waiting room. He's a fighter, but I have him sedated for now. I will be there soon," the librarian said. She reached into the library and pulled someone into the hall.

Jenny gasped. Josh pushed her away and turned back to watch. A blindfolded man leaned against the librarian as if he were partly asleep.

The man moved his head. Even with the blindfold, Josh knew it was Mr. Ott.

CHAPTER

→ 3 ←

Follow That Sub

The substitute took Mr. Ott by the arm and led him toward the stairs. He stumbled at the first step, but walked the rest of the way without falling.

Miss Fable smiled. "Everything is working out just fine. We'll be done before anyone can stop us."

She walked down the hall toward the office.

"Come on!" Josh said, grabbing his sister's hand.

Jenny squeezed her brother's hand. "Poor Mr. Ott. What will they do with him?"

Josh led Jenny to the stairs. "Nothing if we can stop them. We have to hurry before we lose them," he said.

Jenny glared at him. "I know that. Stop trying to big brother me. I'm older, you know. By ten whole minutes."

They ran up the stairs. There was only one class on the second floor. Music. Next door was the teacher's lounge.

Josh could see the substitute and Mr. Ott standing in front of the door to the lounge. The substitute knocked slowly. When the door opened, she went inside and pulled Mr. Ott after her.

Jenny walked past the music room. "Come on," she said. "But be quiet with your big, loud feet or they'll hear us."

Josh pointed to the music room. "Not with all that noise." Josh grinned. From inside it sounded like monkeys beating on drums, clashing cymbals, and banging on a piano.

Josh and Jenny ducked in front of the door to the teacher's lounge. Josh peeked in the window.

Inside were several substitutes, but no regular teachers.

"I don't see Mr. Ott," Josh whispered.

Then he saw a door closing as two people walked inside. The outside of the door was marked PRIVATE! DO NOT ENTER!

Then all of the substitutes went into the private room. When the last one was inside, Josh said, "Come on!"

They hurried into the teacher's lounge. It looked like a normal room for grown-ups to have lunch. There was a coffee pot, a microwave, chairs, a table, and a refrigerator.

"They went through here," Josh said, opening the other door.

The first thing he saw were clothes hanging on either side. Instead of left to right like in a regular closet, they hung in two long rows. There were enough gray pants and blue shirts for substitutes to fill the school.

They moved farther into the room. Jenny backed into a small table, turned, and squealed.

"Eyes!" she shouted.

Josh bent down and looked at a big jar. The jar looked back at him.

Jenny tapped the jar. The floating balls bobbed up and down in a purple liquid. "Oh wait, it's green contacts on white balls," she said.

"Weird!" said Josh.

They moved around the room until they came to a wall. "This is just a big closet," Josh said.

"Where did they go?" Jenny asked.

Josh put his hands against the wall, hoping it was an illusion. It wasn't. He moved the clothes around. Then he saw a metal bar sticking out of the wall. A lever.

He grabbed it and pushed it down. With a WHOOSH, the back wall slid open. Bright lights filled a large room.

Josh held his sister's hand and stepped inside. He blinked several times. He held his other hand over his eyes until he was used to the bright lights.

This was the strangest room he'd ever seen. The room was round with no windows or corners. It was a room of doors. No furniture, just doors.

"Wow!" Jenny said.

Besides the door they came in, there were eight colored doors and a simple brown one. Josh shook his head. There were orange, pink, purple, blue, green, yellow, silver, and red doors. Each one had a gold knob and no window. The only normal looking door was the brown one.

"So many colors," Jenny said. "Why would anyone have a big, round room with nothing but doors?"

"What do you think is behind them?" Josh said. He walked over to the silver door. It was his favorite color. It reminded him of science fiction movies with shiny spacesuits and ships and monsters with spinning eyes.

Jenny went to the purple door. Josh knew she would like that one. Her bedroom was decorated in purple everything.

"There could be anything behind here," she said. She reached a hand toward the door, then jumped back and yelled, "Ouch!"

"What happened?" Josh asked.

Jenny rubbed her hand. "It shocked me. And I didn't even touch it."

They stared at the doors for several minutes.

Josh took a deep breath. They couldn't just stand around looking at the doors. He reached toward the knob on the orange door. "We have to find Mr. Ott and get to the police."

Jenny screamed. "No, Josh!"

But Josh grabbed the knob and turned. There was no electric shock. Instead, a loud siren sounded in the room and red lights flashed where the bright white ones had been before.

Josh tugged on the door but it wouldn't open. Jenny ran toward the brown door. She grabbed the handle and pulled. It opened to a hallway. Josh pushed her through and ran in behind her. Sirens echoed in the hall.

Jenny covered her ears as she ran.

"Which way?" she shouted. "What if we never find Mr. Ott? What if we're lost here forever? Maybe it's a giant maze and we just walk in circles."

Josh glared at his sister. Sometimes when Jenny was scared or upset, she talked like someone had fast-forwarded her mouth.

Josh stared ahead of them. There were three different halls. They looked exactly the same. They were all long, with one door at the end.

"Left one!" Josh shouted.

Josh's ears hurt from the sirens. They were louder than before. He wondered if students in the school could hear it. When he reached the end of the hall and opened the door, a substitute stared back at him.

CHAPTER

→≫ 4 ≪←

Green Eyes and Ham!

"Yaah!" Josh yelled. He backed away as the substitute reached a hand for him. Her fingers twitched and she smiled that creepy smile.

"Go back to the middle hall!" Jenny shouted as more substitutes poured through the doorway.

They ran back to where the three halls met and hurried down the middle one. Jenny pushed against the door at the end of the hall. It opened into the cafeteria.

Josh followed her inside and closed the door behind him. All around them, cafeteria workers opened cans, pulled biscuits from the oven, and slapped fish sticks onto trays. They didn't speak a word.

"How did we end up in the cafeteria?" Jenny whispered.

Josh shook his head. Josh thought one of the cooks would yell at them for being in the cafeteria. It wasn't until they walked to the other side that all the workers turned and stared at them.

Jenny gasped. "They all have green eyes!"

The cooks yelled in unison, "They are here! They are here!"

Josh and Jenny grabbed ladles off the wall. They swung them back and forth and backed through the exit door.

"I'll never buy food in the cafeteria again," Jenny said.

Josh held his stomach. "Imagine finding one of those green contacts floating in your beef stew surprise or laying on a slice of ham. Ugh."

"Mmelp! Mmelp!"

Josh spun around at the sound. "What's that?"

"It sounds like someone trying to yell," Jenny said.

Josh and Jenny zigzagged through a hall that bent and twisted. Then they saw the librarian, two substitutes, and Mr. Ott. One of the substitutes had his hand over their teacher's mouth.

"Mr. Ott must have woken up. He's trying to get away," Josh said.

Josh and Jenny moved fast, but they were careful to be as quiet as they could. The farther they walked, the narrower the hall got.

"It's like a fun house or something," Jenny said as she squeezed through.

Josh sucked in his breath. They were sliding sideways through the hall. Ahead of them, everyone disappeared.

"Hey, where did they go?" Josh asked.

Jenny pointed. "I saw them. A door slid open in the wall and they went through."

Josh was tired of weird hallways, strange doors, and green eyes. He followed Jenny down the hall. She stopped in front of a spot that looked just like the rest of the wall. She looked up and down, pushing against the wall until Josh heard a click and a part of it slid into the ceiling.

"I wonder if these hidden places have always been at Harding," Josh said when the door closed behind them. "I feel like we're in a Star Trek movie."

From down the hall, they heard a clicking noise.

"What's that?" Josh asked. "Sounds like a giant cricket."

Jenny cocked her head. She loved anything to do with bugs. "No, not a cricket."

"Where did they go?" Josh asked. He didn't want a lecture on the sound a cricket makes.

"I don't know," Jenny said. "We need to get out of here and tell Mom and Dad about this. And call the police. And the FBI. And the president."

Josh agreed. Maybe it wasn't such a great idea to do this by themselves. Maybe they were in real trouble. Maybe they'd never get out or the librarian would turn them into something weird and send substitute Josh and Jennys back to class.

They followed the clicking sound. Instead of getting louder, it seemed farther away. Then it stopped.

"Well, that was useless," Jenny said.

Josh saw another door. This one had a small window. He watched until he saw someone move past it. Finally, a face peered through it. It was the librarian. She moved away.

Josh heard the clicking sound again.

A man shouted, "Let me out of here! Do you hear me? What's wrong with you, Shirley?"

"That's Mr. Ott," Jenny whispered. They slipped back around a corner and waited.

From downstairs somewhere, an alarm sounded. The door opened and Miss Fable ran out, the two substitutes behind her. The clicking sound got louder. It was the substitutes. Their tattoos turned in circles and made the noise. The librarian pressed buttons on a keypad and locked the door. She turned and ran down the other end of the hall. The subs followed her.

"This is our chance," Josh said. "But we have to hurry, before they come back."

Jenny was already running toward the door.

Josh reached the door just as Mr. Ott looked through the window.

Jenny screamed. Josh ran up to her and looked at their teacher.

Mr. Ott stared at them with green eyes.

Chapter

5

Rescue

"Get me out of here!" Mr. Ott shouted.

Josh shook his head. "We want to, but you have green eyes. Just like the substitutes."

Mr. Ott smiled. It wasn't a creepy smile. Just his regular one.

"I was born with green eyes." He reached down, pulled out his wallet, and shoved his driver's license against the window.

Josh and Jenny bent forward. The picture showed green eyes.

Josh gave Mr. Ott a thumbs-up. He grabbed the doorknob, but it wouldn't turn.

"Uh-oh, there's a keypad here."

Jenny shoved him aside. "I've got this."

Josh and Jenny's parents said she had the eyes of an eagle. Josh and Jenny made a great detective team. Fly-ears and Eagle-eyes. Josh watched while she pressed the numbers 4-4-2-8.

Josh turned the doorknob again. Nothing.

"Hold on, let me think," Jenny said. This time she pressed 4-4-2-6.

Josh heard a click. He tried again, and the door opened. "Great job, Jenny!"

Mr. Ott rushed into the hall. "I don't know how you found me, but I'm very grateful. Something strange is going on in this school."

Josh told him about how they'd been following him and the librarian, the substitutes chasing them, and the weird cafeteria workers.

"Our cousin goes to Bluebonnet Elementary, and he started noticing some substitutes there, too," Jenny added.

Mr. Ott squeezed their shoulders. "We have to get out of here and get help."

"The police, right?" Jenny asked.

Mr. Ott shrugged. "Well, something like that."

Josh and Jenny led the way, turning and twisting down the hall.

"Do you know where we're going, Josh?" Mr. Ott asked.

"No, but I know where we've been and it wasn't good," Josh said.

He stopped, his shoes squeaking on the floor. In front of them was a spiral staircase. It reminded him of the one his family had climbed when they visited a lighthouse on vacation.

"Wow, look at that," Josh said.

Jenny pointed at the stairs. "It goes down, and I think that's the way we need to go to get back to the regular part of the school."

Mr. Ott nodded. He started down the stairs, with Josh and Jenny following. The metal stairs were

noisy. Their shoes made heavy *clang clang* sounds.

The stairs curled and twisted until Josh felt like he was on a roller coaster. The metal shook with the weight of three people.

They passed a section where the walls were all glass. Inside, Josh saw beds and machines and more glasses of floating green contacts. One room had red wigs hanging on hooks.

"What do you think is going on here, Mr. Ott?" Jenny asked. "You're a teacher, so you should know everything about the school."

"Teachers don't know everything," Mr. Ott said. "I'm new, and every time teachers complain or start asking questions around here, they disappear."

"Do the substitutes talk to any of the regular teachers?" Josh asked. He missed one of the metal steps and caught himself before he fell. Where was the end? The school had only two floors. Where did these stairs go?

"They only speak to us to ask questions," Mr. Ott said. "Just like with the students. They seem curious and a bit confused. The students complain about all the questions they ask everywhere they go."

"And what about those tattoos?" Jenny asked. "How could every substitute look almost the same and have tattoos that sometimes make noise and move?"

Mr. Ott said, "I've tried to ask them questions in the break room, but they just stare at me or walk out of the room. We used to keep supplies in the closet, paper plates and plastic forks for our lunch. But suddenly it was locked and none of us could get in. Principal Rodriguez even seemed surprised. She called a locksmith to open it, but after he checked in at the office, no one saw him again."

"Wow," Jenny said. "And it looks like Miss Fable is in charge of this weirdness."

Mr. Ott nodded. "After lunch I went back to the classroom, and she was waiting at my door. She told me to come with her. When I told her my students would be back soon, she said not to worry. She grabbed me, pushed something into my arm like a shot without a needle. That's the last thing I remember until finding myself blindfolded in that room where you found me."

Josh shook his head. How many real teachers were left now? And what was the librarian doing with them? Even more important, what would she do to him and Jenny if she caught them?

Josh took another step and realized he was on the last step of the stairs. Finally, he stepped onto the floor. He didn't think he'd ever climb up a lighthouse again, not if it had stairs like that.

After Jenny stepped off the stairs, Josh could still hear the *clang* of footsteps. He looked up to see a group of substitutes moving quickly down the stairs.

"Run!" Jenny shouted.

Josh wondered what would happen if they didn't run? What if they waited and questioned the subs? He thought about all those green-eyed, red-haired, creepy smiling substitutes. He ran.

This time, he and Jenny followed Mr. Ott. After a few minutes, the teacher stopped.

"Sssh, do you hear that?" Mr. Ott asked.

"What?" Jenny asked.

Josh listened. "I heard it. That sounds like balls bouncing."

He heard shouting and a whistle. They were under the school gym somehow. He wished he were in there playing basketball or doing push-ups instead of hiding from deranged substitutes and an evil librarian.

Mr. Ott snapped his fingers. "I heard Miss Fable say something into a walkie-talkie to one of her assistants about securing the control room whenever classes were in the gym. She said to turn down the volume."

"Look, over there," Jenny said. She hurried to a bright red door. It had a glass handle.

Josh watched as his sister pulled the handle up, then down. The door opened. Miss Fable must not have expected anyone to get this far into the secret place. Jenny turned and smiled. She pulled the door open wider.

Jenny gasped. She walked into the room before Josh could yell at her. Mr. Ott rushed in behind her.

Josh ran to the door. He had a feeling they were finally going to get some answers.

Chapter
→ 6 ←

Computer Spying

Josh had never seen so many computers in one place. The room was as big as the gym above. There were rows and rows of long desks. At each desk was a computer. But not like the ones in the library or the one at his house.

These were shiny, silver oblong boxes. When Josh reached out to touch one, it hummed against his hand. The metal was cold and hard. They looked like bigger versions of the wrist cell phones the substitutes wore.

Mr. Ott whistled. "I've never seen anything like them." He sat at one of the desks.

Josh and Jenny stood behind their teacher. The keyboard was even weirder than the computer. It didn't have the alphabet and number keys. Instead, each large key had a picture, just like the tattoos. A butterfly, fish, frog, and more.

"Look, Mr. Ott," Jenny said. "There's one with a ladybug. The substitute in your room had that tattoo."

Mr. Ott pressed the key with a ladybug on it.

Across the room a screen appeared on the wall.

"It's our class!" Josh shouted.

Marvin Green passed sheets of paper to each student. Mr. Ott pressed an arrow key. The screen zoomed in on the paper on Glenda Davis's desk.

The paper was full of questions. But they weren't about the book they'd just finished reading in class or about long division or anything else they had been learning since school started.

It was a list of questions:

1. How does your teacher learn about the subjects she or he teaches you?
2. What is the most important thing a child of this world learns in school?
3. Does your teacher get punished if you do not learn correctly?
4. How would you learn if you did not have a teacher?

The questions continued down the paper. They were about teachers, teaching, and what students had learned about their government, space, survival, home life, and more.

The substitute in Mr. Ott's room stood quietly. As the students answered the questions, she would stop them and ask them to read their answers out loud.

She talked into her phone before asking another question. If the kid she asked did not understand the question, she did not explain it. Instead, she asked the same question to another student.

Josh went to a different computer. He pressed a button with a rabbit on it.

Another screen popped up next to the one from Mr. Ott's room. It was a kindergarten class. A substitute sat in the middle of a circle of children. She turned to each one and asked a question.

"Why do your parents make you go to school? Why do you listen to your teacher? Why do you hug her? What is the importance of painting with your fingers?"

The little kids looked confused. Their eyes were wide. Their lips quivered. They moved away when the substitute leaned toward them.

Josh started pressing more buttons. The walls were soon covered with screens showing rooms where the substitutes had taken over. None of them was teaching. None of the kids looked happy.

"I don't know what's going on, but we have to call for help," Mr. Ott said. "Look for a phone."

"You look by the computers, Josh," said Jenny. "I'll search around the walls."

"If you find a phone, let me do the talking," said Mr. Ott. "It's going to sound weird enough as it is, but at least I'm a teacher."

Josh ran to the door they had come in. He got on his knees and crawled around the floor looking for an old-fashioned phone jack. But there was nothing. When he got back to the door, he stood and walked around the wall again to look higher.

"Nope, nothing. Not even an electric plug," Josh said.

Jenny walked back to them. "I didn't find any kind of phone either. I bet they just use their cell phones."

Mr. Ott tapped his finger against his chin. "You would think there might be one main phone here, but you are probably right, Jenny."

Suddenly the screens disappeared from the wall. All except one. It stretched to cover the whole wall. Loud screeches echoed around the room. The face of a substitute moved in close to the camera and she stared into the lens. Her starfish tattoo crawled all over her face, then stopped on her nose.

She blinked at the camera and screamed, "Intruders!"

The camera lens shook when she grabbed it.

The wall went blank.

CHAPTER
→» 7 «←

Captured

"Hey! What happened? Did you touch something?" Jenny asked.

Josh shook his head. "How could I? We're all standing here together."

The screen on the wall slowly faded in again. The camera lens was crooked, but they could still see the whole classroom.

"Why did she do that? I've never seen one of the substitutes scream like that. Or show any emotion," Jenny said.

Josh wished they allowed students to carry cell phones, but Harding rules were strict about that. If only they could call the police or someone for help.

"Mr. Ott, do you have a cell phone" Josh asked.

"I did, but when they locked me in that room, I checked and it was gone," Mr. Ott said.

Jenny shook her finger at the monitor as if someone would see her. "This isn't nice, letting us kids get trapped. And scaring kids in class. And having teachers with clown-red hair. Don't they know how many kids are scared of clowns?"

The substitute kept staring at the camera. "It's like she knows we're here, " said Jenny.

"These substitutes seem to be able to communicate with one another," said Mr. Ott. "Maybe it's through these main computers and those strange tattoos."

After a moment, the substitute smiled at the camera.

"I hate that smile," Josh said.

Jenny tried pushing other keys on the computer in front of her, but the image on the wall didn't change.

"I wish this keyboard made sense," she said. "My dad showed me lots of things about hacking into computer systems, but this one is too weird."

Mr. Ott raised his eyebrows. "Your dad teaches you how to hack?"

"Only simple stuff," said Josh. "Jenny likes to show off sometimes."

The substitute on the screen tapped her finger against her ear. "I can hear them talking. But you had better hurry before they get away."

Then the wall went blank again.

"We'd better get out of here," Josh said.

Jenny nodded.

"It seems Substitute Starfish has located our curious students and runaway teacher. I was afraid this would happen if we didn't move quickly," a voice said.

Josh turned. Behind them, the room was filled with silent substitutes. Miss Fable stood in front of them.

"I wish you hadn't found this room and your teacher, children," she said. "We will have to do something to keep you from ruining our plans."

The Ending Is Up2U!

If you think Josh, Jenny, and Mr. Ott take a substitute's cell phone and call for help, turn to page 52.

→ OR ←

If you think Josh, Jenny, and Mr. Ott decide to fight back and get away from Miss Fable and the substitutes, turn to page 63.

→ OR ←

If you think Josh, Jenny, and Mr. Ott confront Miss Fable and demand answers about what is happening, turn to page 72.

ENDING

→ 1 ←

Creating Chaos

Josh moved closer to his sister. Mr. Ott walked toward Miss Fable. The substitutes spread slowly into a circle around them.

"Leave these children alone," Mr. Ott said. "Whatever you're doing, it's over now. You are caught."

Miss Fable laughed. The substitutes smiled their creepy smiles.

"Caught? You are the ones who are caught," she said.

Josh stared at the strange phones on the substitutes' wrists. He ran to the nearest substitute and pulled the phone from her.

"I've got you now!" Josh yelled. He punched in 9-1-1. All of the substitutes' phones began ringing. He quickly dialed his dad's cell. Again, the phones around him rang.

Miss Fable shook her head. "Sorry, but those phones can only be sent to the others. They do not have outside lines."

Josh threw the phone on the floor. It exploded into little pieces, leaving a puff of smoke.

Jenny walked toward the librarian. Josh wanted to stop her, but his sister couldn't be stopped when she was upset.

"Miss Fable, I always loved going into the library," Jenny said. "You helped me find lots of books for projects and just for fun. Why are you doing this?"

The librarian said, "I was good at being a librarian. But that's not my real job. And, my name isn't Miss Fable. It is Dr. Edith Fablestine."

Josh's mouth dropped. "Dr. Fablestine? But you are a famous scientist." He thought for a moment.

He remembered reading about her in one of his science fiction magazines. "You were working on an important project, but something happened, didn't it?"

Dr. Fablestine nodded. "Yes, I was nominated for the Carnegie Science Award for my work with robots. I created specialized robots to replace human workers. Policemen, firemen, doctors, and nurses."

"And teachers?" Jenny asked.

"Yes. Humans aren't perfect. We have too many emotions and make too many mistakes. People cost money. Robots don't worry about being paid. They can be shut down when not used. No homes, food, or medical needs," Dr. Fablestine said.

Josh snapped his fingers. "I remember. There were police robots in Texas. Their power source got hit by lightning. And then . . ."

"Then, they went out of control," Mr. Ott said. "They gave everyone tickets for everything. They filled the jails with people who didn't commit crimes. They caused chaos."

The scientist nodded. "And someone got hurt. I was fired and my name was ruined."

The substitutes surrounding them moved a little closer. Their green eyes glowed.

"I just had to try again. I thought the robots would make better teachers. But all they want to do is ask questions," Dr. Fablestine said. "And lately, they have begun ignoring my commands."

"What is that room of glowing doors?" Jenny asked.

Dr. Fablestine went to one of the computers. She pressed a button and a screen popped up on the wall showing the room of doors. She pressed another button and all of the doors opened.

Josh's eyes went wide. Dozens of red-haired, green-eyed substitutes marched through the doors.

"It's an army of creepy substitutes!" Jenny screamed.

Dr. Fablestine nodded. "I have them in two other schools. They could easily take over all the schools. But I have failed again. The children don't like them. Especially the little ones."

"Why do they have tattoos?" Josh asked.

Dr. Fablestine sighed. "It was supposed to be a way to make them less frightening. By using familiar symbols I thought students would like them better. But they are still afraid."

The substitutes in the room moved much closer until there was no break between them.

"What's going on?" Josh asked.

Dr. Fablestine shook her head. "They are out of control. I'm afraid there is nothing we can do."

Josh remembered a science fiction movie he saw once. Crazy robots were taking over the world. Until one guy did something.

Josh took off one of his size eleven shoes. His sister called them boats. He shouted, "Miss Fable! I mean, Dr. Fablestine. Which is the main computer?"

She pointed across the room. "That one in the corner. The red one."

Josh stood on tiptoes to look over the shoulder of a substitute. He hadn't noticed the one red computer in the room before.

"I have to get to it," Josh said. "I need a distraction."

He glanced at Jenny. She grinned. Sometimes, they used a special plan to distract his parents when they'd broken something or tracked mud in the house. Jenny could be very annoying when she tried.

Jenny stood in front of one of the substitutes. "Why do you all have red hair? Is red your favorite?"

She walked to the next substitute. "Do you like having green eyes? What's your favorite color? Is it blue, like the sky? Or would you rather have brown eyes, like the color of mud? Do you know how to make mud?"

She turned to the next one, "Mud is a funny word, isn't it? Isn't mud messy? Would you play in the mud with me?"

As she moved to each robot, the one she had just questioned followed her. They all began talking at once, asking her questions about hair, eyes, colors, and mud. Soon there was a large gap in the circle of substitutes.

Josh limped across the room with his shoe in his hand. He stood in front of the red computer and raised the shoe.

"Don't destroy them!" Dr. Fablestine shouted.

"Do it!" yelled Mr. Ott.

Dr. Fablestine pushed one of the substitutes. "Stop him!"

They all turned and moved toward Josh, even the ones Jenny was questioning. Josh slammed his shoe into the computer. He hit it again and again. Sparks shot out of the computer. The wall screens flickered on and off, flashing pictures of the classrooms with substitutes.

Josh hit it until smoke poured from the computer. He backed away as Mr. Ott grabbed a fire extinguisher hanging beside the door and sprayed it over the computer.

Josh turned as the substitutes reached him and Mr. Ott. They stretched their hands toward them. Then, with a screech and a popping noise, they stopped. Their green eyes weren't glowing any longer.

"Look at the screens!" Jenny yelled.

Josh looked up and saw that in every classroom the substitutes had stopped. They didn't move as the students ran to touch them. Some of the kids ran out of the rooms yelling. Others applauded. The few teachers who were left in the school came into the rooms and moved the children away from the substitutes.

"It's over," Josh said.

Dr. Fablestine covered her face with her hands. "You've ruined everything. I could've repaired them. School systems everywhere would've paid me a fortune. I would have been rich!"

Mr. Ott stepped in front of her. He reached into his pocket and pulled out a pair of handcuffs. With a quick motion, he put them on her wrists.

"You are under arrest, Dr. Fablestine."

Josh stared at Jenny. He poked Mr. Ott's arm.

"Can a teacher arrest someone?"

"No," Mr. Ott said, "But an undercover FBI agent can. We've been watching Dr. Fablestine for a long time now. I started teaching here when we discovered she was your librarian. I had to find out what she was doing. But I didn't expect to be captured."

He shook Josh's and Jenny's hands.

"You have been a great help to your school and your country. You rescued me and destroyed the robots. Now we know how to take care of the ones at the other schools. And Dr. Fablestine will not be creating any robots from prison."

Josh looked around the strange room filled with broken robots and computers. He stared at the shoe in his hand.

"Well, Jenny, you can't ever make fun of my big shoes again," he said.

Jenny grinned. "And don't say I ask too many annoying questions ever again."

They followed Mr. Ott and the librarian-mad scientist out of the room.

Josh stopped in the hallway and grabbed his sister's arm. "Uh-oh, who's going to be our substitute when Mr. Ott goes back to the FBI?"

Jenny's eyes opened wide. Then she started to giggle. Josh laughed with her. As long as their substitute didn't have red hair and green eyes, they would be okay.

Ending

→ 2 ←

Surrender

Josh moved closer to his sister. Miss Fable wasn't getting them without a fight. Mr. Ott stood in front of both of them.

The librarian stared at them. One of her eyes suddenly turned black. She bent down to pick something off the floor. "Silly contacts. What a ridiculous idea you humans have, pushing something onto your eye." She blinked several times until the other contact fell into her hand.

Josh stared into her giant black eyes.

"Us humans?" Jenny asked.

Miss Fable reached up and pulled off her hair. Then she pulled off her face.

Josh gasped. Jenny screamed. She pointed at the librarian. "Hey, you aren't Miss Fable!"

The librarian nodded. Her head seemed to flatten out, looking more like a hammerhead shark head. She had a wide mouth. Josh was glad it wasn't filled with giant sharp teeth.

"No, I'm not your librarian. My name is too difficult to say in your language. Just call me Your Highness."

Josh realized he was holding his breath. She was an alien, a real live alien. All around them the substitutes removed their fake hair and faces. Dozens of hammerhead shark aliens surrounded them.

Jenny asked, "Your Highness? Why would we call you that? Who do you think you are, the queen of the universe?"

The alien-librarian said, "That is my plan. I am queen on my planet. If you all do what we ask, I can be a good queen to you. Or, a not so good one."

Josh didn't know whether to be excited or scared. He'd always wanted to meet an alien. Now, the room was full of them. The school was full of them. So were other schools.

The alien queen snapped her fingers. Six of the aliens moved toward them. Two grabbed Josh's arms and held them tight. Two more grabbed Jenny's and Mr. Ott's arms. Josh looked down and saw the alien's hands were like lobster claws.

The aliens dragged them to chairs near a row of computers. They pressed a button on the chairs and metal bars popped up and over their arms.

"Let the children go," Mr. Ott said.

The alien queen smiled. Josh liked it even less than when the substitutes smiled.

"You will not be harmed. But you cannot leave until all the teachers have been replaced in the schools I am now controlling."

Josh tugged his arms against the metal bands, but he couldn't move them. He glanced at Jenny. She winked at him and wiggled her skinny arms. Josh quietly watched her squeeze one hand through the band. He would never call her Spaghetti Arms again.

"So, why the substitutes? Why sneak into schools? Don't aliens go to the leaders of other planets?" Josh thought if he could just keep her distracted, Jenny might get away.

"Your Highness, this one is escaping!" Mr. Ott shouted.

Josh stared at his teacher. One of the substitutes grabbed Jenny just as she pulled free of the bands and leaped off her chair.

"What are you doing?" Jenny screamed at her teacher. "I almost got away."

The bands on Mr. Ott opened. He rubbed his wrists. "They are too dangerous. I don't want to see you get hurt."

The alien queen waved her claw hands and Josh was suddenly free. Before he could run, two substitutes grabbed his arms. Jenny kicked her substitute's leg and jerked away. Josh glared at Mr. Ott. Why didn't he let Jenny get away?

"You mustn't try to run," their once-librarian said. "We are too many. We have been here on this planet for many years. Waiting."

Josh wondered how many aliens were living on his street? In his town? In the world?

"Come," the former librarian said. "I'll explain in the Room of Doors."

Josh and Jenny walked as close together as the alien substitutes would let them. Josh thought about how long it took to get to the computer room from the room full of doors. But the alien queen took them down a different hall and into an elevator. Only the alien queen, Mr. Ott, Josh, and Jenny were inside when the doors shut.

Josh's stomach seemed to drop as they moved quickly up. When the door opened, they were again surrounded by different colored doors. The substitutes were gone.

"Through each of those doors is a teleport that takes us to our ships above your Earth," the alien queen said. She went to a pink door, turned the knob, and opened it.

Josh saw darkness, then millions of stars. The alien queen stepped out the door. Josh expected her to float away screaming. But she disappeared.

Seconds later, she was standing in the doorway again and walked inside.

"Why do you all wear the same disguises?" Jenny asked. "And what about the tattoos? Whoever heard of aliens with tattoos."

"It is easier for us to know where we all are," the queen explained. "And we thought if we were average looking, it would be less frightening. The tattoos are devices like your cameras."

"Average looking?" Jenny said. "Humans look and act different. And we don't all have tattoos on our faces."

"It's creepy," Josh said. "I guess the phones sent information back to your ship?"

"Ships," the alien queen corrected him.

"Where are our teachers?" Jenny asked.

"Aboard our ships, teaching our people. Our planet died, and we must begin again. We have monitored your schools and found many hardworking teachers," the queen said. "While they teach our people about human life, our substitutes are here learning even more about your planet."

"From kids?" Josh said. "We don't know everything."

"We are learning from many places on your planet. Government, entertainment, and even family. We have found it is often easiest to understand things one does not understand by learning from children. If we are to know more about our new planet and how to achieve surrender, we must learn simply," the alien said.

Josh had a bad feeling. "Which new planet?"

The alien smiled as the doors opened and more aliens came inside the room. They too smiled.

"Earth. This will be our new planet."

Jenny's eyes went wide. Josh looked to their teacher for help.

With one quick movement, he removed his fake hair and face. He looked at them with green eyes in his hammerhead face. He bowed to the queen.

"Please greet our invasion commander," the alien queen said.

The commander cocked his huge head. "I'm sorry I had to lie to you. Even though you are human, I like you both. And there are a few of us who were born with green eyes, so I didn't lie about that."

Jenny moved closer to the alien commander. She blinked her green eyes at him, then smiled at Josh. Jenny had the darkest green eyes he'd ever seen. Except for their mom's eyes. They were even darker green.

Jenny took the alien commander's claw in her own hand. Josh wondered what it would be like being ruled by hammerhead shark people.

ENDING

→ 3 ←

Strangers in Red Wigs

Josh backed up against the computers. Jenny ran toward the librarian. She stood in front of Miss Fable and folded her arms. "So, what's the big deal? Who are you anyway? And what happened to all the teachers? We don't like these substitutes at all. They are scary. Are they robots? Aliens?"

Miss Fable smiled at Jenny. "You ask a lot of questions, young lady."

Josh ran to his sister's side. "Not as many questions as those substitutes."

Miss Fable held out her hands. "Okay, you're right. Something is going on. And no, the substitutes aren't robots or aliens. They are teachers."

Jenny shook her head. "They aren't teachers here. We've never seen them before. And they don't act like our regular teachers."

Miss Fable snapped her fingers. The substitutes moved into a circle around them. They smiled their creepy smiles. Then Miss Fable snapped her fingers twice. The substitutes blinked and shook their heads as if they just woke from a long sleep.

"Where am I?" one asked.

"Did we succeed?" another asked.

"The program was a complete success, thanks to these two. I was beginning to wonder if anyone would be brave enough to question us," Miss Fable said.

Josh walked around the circle of substitutes. They were talking and smiling. Not creepy, weird smiles, but happy ones.

"Go ahead," Miss Fable said. "Remove your disguises."

All the substitutes pulled off their red wigs and removed their green contacts. Then, they peeled off the tattoos from their faces.

"They look like normal people now," Jenny said. "Everyone is different."

"Of course," Miss Fable said. "They've been hypnotized to act the same. They agreed to it. The tattoos are special computers that allow us to film and monitor the students' responses."

One of the substitutes handed Mr. Ott a silver notebook. He read a moment then said, "It seems your story is true, Miss Fable. But why? And why didn't you tell me and the other teachers?"

"I'm sorry, you should have been included in the program," Miss Fable said. "Things moved faster than I anticipated."

Jenny folded her arms. "I don't like this at all. I still think we should call the police."

"Why were you kidnapping me?" asked Mr. Ott.

Miss Fable pointed at the substitutes. "You weren't being kidnapped. We were going to ask you to join us, but you got too upset and wouldn't listen."

Josh had heard enough. He wanted a real answer. "You keep talking about a program. What is it? And why do you say it was a success thanks to me and Jenny?"

"Come over here and let me explain," said Miss Fable.

Josh, Jenny, and Mr. Ott followed her to a large, red computer. She sat down and pressed several keys. On the wall, a screen showed the Room of Doors.

"I'm part of a research team studying how students learn. The idea was to have strange teachers come in and see how much the students were learning by asking them questions. The test was to end when students, not just teachers, became upset and curious enough to search for and find out what was happening in their school."

Jenny frowned. "You had everyone scared of these substitutes. Why couldn't you tell us what was happening?"

Miss Fable shook her head. "It wouldn't be a test if you knew ahead of time."

"Where do those doors lead?" Mr. Ott asked.

Miss Fable pressed a few keys on the computer. The red door swung open and a camera zoomed through the door. The door opened to a parking lot with a red helicopter waiting.

"We move teachers from one school to another once they agree to our plan. They become the substitutes for the other schools," Miss Fable explained.

Josh groaned. "I still don't think it's right. You tricked all of us."

Mr. Ott looked up from the notebook. "I think Miss Fable has been part of such programs for a long time now," he said.

"We've been trying to perfect our studies for years," she explained. "This is our fourth year. Your school is one of three in this state."

Josh took the notebook when Mr. Ott held it out to him. He read the page Mr. Ott showed him.

"So, the idea is to find students who question what's going on around them?" asked Josh. "Students who think for themselves?"

"Yes, that's it," Miss Fable said. "We want creative minds. We want students who think beyond the normal classroom studies. There are about two dozen students around the country who have completed this challenge. They meet once a month to brainstorm ideas for better ways to learn."

"Wow," Jenny said. "I'm glad it wasn't something bad."

"Come with me to the Room of Doors," said Miss Fable. "You can greet your returning teachers."

Mr. Ott walked between Josh and Jenny. "I guess my surprise wasn't as big as this one."

Josh couldn't think of anything better than meeting with kids from around the country to plan creative school programs.

"What was the project?" Jenny asked.

Mr. Ott winked at them. "Substituting the cafeteria food with our own pizza business one day a week for six weeks."

Josh didn't want to talk about substituting anything for awhile. A long while.

Josh and Jenny walked into the Room of Doors, just as their missing teachers came through. They all had blond hair and blue eyes. This time, the tattoos were on their hands.

Miss Fable smiled. "Now, if the three of you will just go through the orange door, you will be assigned to your new school for the rest of the semester."

"What new school?" Jenny asked.

"Uh-oh, it's the two-part test with a twist," whispered Mr. Ott.

Josh groaned.

Jenny took a deep breath. "It looks like we're going to be substitute kids for awhile."

The three followed Miss Fable through the orange door. As they stepped into the helicopter, they were each given a red wig and a set of light green contacts.

WRITE YOUR OWN ENDING

There were three endings to choose from in *The Substitutes*. Did you find the ending you wanted from the story? Or did you want something different to happen? Now it is your turn! Write the ending you would like to see. Be creative!